Aug 9—Fog

Aug 9—Fog

KATHRYN SCANLAN

MCD 

Farrar, Straus and Giroux | New York

MCD
Farrar, Straus and Giroux
120 Broadway, New York 10271

Printed in the United States of America
First edition, 2019

This work was inspired by a diary kept by Cora E. Lacy from 1968 to 1972.

A portion of this text previously appeared, in a different format, in the 2011 edition of *NOON Annual*.

Library of Congress Cataloging-in-Publication Data
Names: Scanlan, Kathryn, 1980– author.
Title: Aug 9—fog / Kathryn Scanlan.
Description: First edition. | New York : MCD, 2019.
Identifiers: LCCN 2018046132 | ISBN 9780374106874 (hardcover)
Classification: LCC PS3619.C2653 A94 2019 | DDC 818/.5403—dc23
LC record available at https://lccn.loc.gov/2018046132

Designed by Richard Oriolo

Our books may be purchased in bulk for promotional, educational, or business use. Please contact your local bookseller or the Macmillan Corporate and Premium Sales Department at 1-800-221-7945, extension 5442, or by e-mail at MacmillanSpecialMarkets@macmillan.com.

www.mcdbooks.com • www.fsgbooks.com
Follow us on Twitter, Facebook, and Instagram at @mcdbooks

10 9 8 7 6 5 4 3 2 1

A NOTE

The text that follows is drawn from a stranger's diary. I acquired the diary fifteen years ago, at a public estate auction. It was among the unsold items. I removed it from a box on its way to the garbage. It looks like garbage—I am surprised it made it to the auction house at all.

It is a small book, approximately the size of my hand, an inch and a quarter thick. The pages have detached from the spine and sit in a solid chunk. The binding is cracked and bandaged with brittle tape.

The diary was at some point submerged, or leaked on—the ink on the bottom third of almost every page has bled (blue, very pretty) and is mostly undecipherable. Front and back covers are pitted with mildew and dirt. The strap that fitted into a brass lock on the front is gone, but the key is sealed in a tiny envelope and tucked inside.

Whenever I handle it, some bits crumble onto my desk.

The diary was a Christmas present to the author from her daughter and son-in-law. The author wrote her full name and address on the front page. She resided in a small Illinois town. She was eighty-six years old when she began recording in it.

The diary chronicles the years 1968 through 1972. Each page is a calendar day, divided into five sections—one for that date for each of the five years. A contemporary vendor of this type of diary claims the format allows you to "travel forward and back in time."

At first I loved only the physicality of the diary—the author's cramped hand, the awkward, artful way she filled the page. I liked its miserable condition. Its position was tenuous—yet here it was. I didn't try to read it. I kept it in a drawer. I assumed it illegible.

But then I did read it—compulsively. I hunched over it, straining my neck. I read it front to back—perhaps a dozen times by now.

As I read, I typed out the sentences that caught my

attention. Then, for ten years, off and on, I played with the sentences I'd pulled. I edited, arranged, and rearranged them into the composition you find here.

At this point—as you might expect—the diarist's voice, her particular use of language, is firmly, intractably lodged in my head. Often I say to myself, "*some hot nite*" or "*flowers coming fast*" or "*grass sure growing*" or "*everything loose is traveling.*"

In fact, I have possessed this work so thoroughly that the diarist has ceased to be an entirely unique, autonomous other to me. I don't picture her. I am her.

The diary has become something like kin—a relation who is also me, myself. I have at times been exasperated with it. I have wondered why I continue to return to it—year after year, draft after draft. Why does it compel me so? Isn't it terribly banal?

Is it like a game I come back to because I've not mastered it?

Is it some kind of sacred text—meant for me alone?

Has it trained me—this inexhaustible textbook—how to choose, contort, order, and cut?

It still moves me, which seems unbelievable.

WINTER

Happy New Year. Brr. Brr. Brr. Alvira a cold. Harold sleep. Few snow flakes in eve. Emma didn't get home.

Clear nice winter day not doing much today. Little squirrel came this A.M. and he sure likes cornbread. Had letter from Bertha she better and contented out there.

I painting. Clouding at noon.

Looking at old books of the church that Martha gave us & pictures, alone all day. Clarence over to see Bayard—he living in the past, other wise he pretty good.

I fixing dark striped dress of Maude's. Maude ate good breakfast, oatmeal, poached eggs, little sausage. Maude ate her dinner pretty good. A letter from Lloyd saying John died the 16th.

27 at noon. 32 at 4. 4 below in nite. Little skift in nite. In eve we sorted them and put in boxes ready to go.

Fine snow rabbit got away. I took pictures of the frost ever where beautiful.

My stomach & bowels not too good in nite. I feel some better this A.M. Didn't find anything wrong with Gary.

No one to church. All home today. D. washing feathers in her pillows.

Sure pretty out. Sure grand out. D. making a new piecrust. All better.

Big snow flakes like little parasols upside down. Ella had Widow's Club to dinner, a delicious fried chicken dinner at Holiday Inn. D. & I out to cemetery little bit.

Bucky came kiddys sick. Maude feeling just fair. Ruth real good. 2 mother red birds here this A.M. Retirement party, they gave her a beautiful clock.

So snowy & bad he came back. Beautiful big red sun dog on the North. D. played her Victrola. Vern working on Doris cupboards.

In P.M. to Burg got my slips. Roads sloppy white rims on trees. That puzzle a humdinger.

Anna Ruth & Bonny came, staid & we had oysters. Pictures. Ruth will have to have the circle tomorrow. Emma not bit good. They are going to decide this P.M. what to do.

Ever where slick. Another beautiful white frost A.M.   eyes got the glimmer.

D. frying chicken. Ice on bird bath.
D. & Vern's anniversary, they got
each other beautiful sweaters. This
grand day my feet tingle.

Finished jig-saw—Niagara Falls.
Very pretty, hard one.

SPRING

D. washing, then they to Burg, D. about her eyes. Wind awful chilly. Tippy sick. Elsie sick. Linda had car accident in P.M.

Janie was lonesome. Thundering. East of us had bad wind blowed cars off road.

Tippy better, wants out. Sits in window, looks out. Fog out. I sure slept. Took a Nytol.

Kind a misty in A.M. I weighed 120 had on blue & new shoes. My feet smelled some.

Mildred papering. Vern took a fish down to Bayard for his birthday. Daffodils and pussy willows out pretty.

Robin on nest today.

Chang gone (the cat). D. set my little hard maple out in front it died. Looking over old clippings. I don't feel any older.

D. & I walked over to Bertha's to see her flowers. We had tea, cookies & candy, legs kind a tingly when we got home.

Started my topsy animal Roy gave me in eve. It will grow long hair. Little showers of rain. Mother's little writing desk. Birdseye maple bed stead & commode.

Windy again today. I am painting. Trees budding. D. hunting up things for her tea.

Terrible windy   everything loose
is traveling.

Stella found a lot of things had been taken, mostly antiques. Grass sure growing. Grass looking green. Blue spruce.

Fire whistle in nite. Steady rain at 8.

He brought us some mush to fry.

Flowers coming fast. All feeling pretty good. Vern making garden, onions & radishes. I painting. D. washing. She hung out some things.

D. & Bucky going to see about head stones. She bought one. Seen ~~8 9 10~~ 11 jets tonite, 2 airplanes & new moon while we were eating supper 6 to 6:45.

D. out to cemetery, her head stone is being put up. We went back out toward eve, stone looks very nice.

Vern got him shirts. Doctors found nothing. Not cloud in sky all day. Mildred little better, she has give up building.

D. & V. got me pretty slippers for Mother's Day. Hard rain last evening sure do lot good. Out to Mother's grave with flowers.

D. washed my head. Fed all my flowers. No dogs in sight today.

Ruth came thru operation. Hiller's house burned. We went out to see what fire had done. Sure clean sweep.

Vern found potato big as hen's egg. Lucile & D. going to river fishing today. Hope it's pretty there.

Ruth come wearing her new red wig. It will look good when we get used to her. Awful murky all day. D. dizzy. Lightning hit & burned Charlie's garage.

SUMMER

A grand rain, it come so nice. Sun looks good. Fire feels good. D. & Vern out on their bicycles.

Vern put me a light in ceiling. Put light down in Vern's lungs. Putting up pictures. Blowed up cooler in eve.

Sorted plastic containers. Over to Maude G. little bit. Took my cactus for her to see the bloom, very pretty dark purple. D. took pictures of it.

Took drive thru timber, turned and come back. Found condemned bridge & we didn't cross it.

All kinds of roads. Dead end roads, roads under construction, cow paths & etc but had good time, a grand day.

My right knee ailing. I washed my head. Janie was hungry.

New neighbors.

Karl all dolled up, put 2 suit cases in trunk of car and away they went. Freddy & wife came here to dinner. She awful small and they are looking for stork.

Vern has fever. Vern better, ate some chicken broth at noon. D. got some very pretty blue rugs for their bedroom. Mother & daughter banquet, we didn't go. Cut some dandelions, cleaned up back porch.

Mr. Overlay over about parakeet.
Mildred sure liked her plane ride.
Vern not working. Kidneys.

Things sure smell fresh. Some hot nite. Flowers beautiful. Ruth brought muskmelons.

D. mowing yard. She made 5 jars peach butter. Peaches white with pink center like we used to have.

Lee called. He found Maude on floor.
Dr. said bring her to hospital.
D. & Vern have gone out there.

Mildred burnt her arm pretty good. Jar broke, she canning tomatoes. Our apples not a bit nice. So spotted. No company today.

D. got a big chunk wax out of right ear. Maude was operated on this A.M. They took out tumor in bladder it was cancer.

Terrible wind storm, D. took me for ride & to see trees down, streets blocked with limbs. Myra picked up 53 sparrows dead.

D. & I out to cemetery decorating. Cemetery looked bad, no mowing. Lightning terrible last nite. Burned out little bed stand light. Vern took treatment on lump in front of ear.

Out to timber for b. berries. Mostly dried up. Got enough for pie when Vern gets home. Bucky got his divorce today.

AUTUMN

I am painting on robin & mountain scene. D. took cactus to basement. Windy little shower leaves coming down fast.

Up had breakfast, left dishes, took long ride out around Round Bottom. Had our lunch & then out to timber. Got 1 bushel of hedge apples. Trees getting real pretty.

D. scalloped oysters. Found another oak tree starting. Misty out. Used a pump on his lungs he was quite bit better.

Leaves sure coming down. Squirrel busy planting buckeyes. We raked leaves, burned some. Buckeye not so pretty this year.

Tippy slept in back porch. He awful good to tell us when he wants out. Tippy sleeping in back porch. Tippy come home around 3. Tippy not home all day.

Mrs. Barber was found last evening.

In eve over to see Mrs. Barber. She looked very nice. Lots beautiful flowers.

I working with stamps. The blocks are a mess. I am going to quit them.

Another picture show brought back many memories. Mother gone '36. Ruth had several stones in the duct. Started my wheel exercise.

D. looking over magazines. Getting along fine without her tooth. New coat. Started painting on my other deer pictures. Didn't take aspirin all day.

Have to put Tippy to sleep. $10.00 on Tippy. They started taking limbs off evergreen. Got lot of burning done. No phone calls or visitors.

D. took Vern to hospital at 4:30. Not operating on Vern, found sugar in blood. I am sewing. Got neck done.

D. took potatoes to cellar A.M. Vern didn't sweat so much. D. painting cupboards yellow inside. I cut off corn & put in freezer 4 plastic boxes. His report not good.

Turning cooler in eve. We had smoked sausages, fried potatoes & onions. Dr. says it's a general breaking up of his body. I am bringing in some flowers.

Found nice teaspoon out in pasture. D. getting Vern's pajamas ready to go back. Over to see Gertrude. She just lays there.

He called. Not so good. Bleeding again. Trying to knit pincushion.

Margaret was confused. Susie's all light up this eve, looks pretty. Vern coughed lot in nite. Vern coughed lot in nite. Vern coughed pretty hard 1 A.M.

D. out tormenting the weeds.

Vern shaved his self toward evening. Rained slower in eve. D. put little fire in furnace. I am cooking apples. He's not vomiting any today.

David's little girl died. In eve out to timber. Got chunks for furnace.

David's baby buried this P.M.

Ice—ice—rainy & fog & freezing & all clouded over. Lee here to dinner. We went home with him. He gave us some things of Maude's. 4 dresses, slippers, hose, etc. Her coat, hat & beads. They were crystal.

WINTER

Got coal $118.52—$32.25 ton. Too dark to do much. Squirrel was here. One spot in my side pretty sore. Other wise I am weak.

Snowflakes this A.M. First I have seen, soon gone. Vern come out to talk for breakfast but couldn't eat. Dr. said he would have his bad days.

Vern sweat bad. D. restless. I slept better. We were in a mess. We took flowers out to cemetery. Mother 121 years.

Tried to paint but too dark. Vern called. Not so good. D. got ready & went. D. home 9:30. Not so good.

Clarence come, brought Vern some beer he wanted. D. staying all night with him.

Not so windy today. I making bread and butter pickles. Alone all day. He is getting weaker.

Vern confused. Vern awful confused.

Vern confused one of the girls with D.

Vern bad nite. Vern bad.

Vern took worse. Passed away before D. got there. Seemed to just sleep away.

Some one here off & on thru day

Such a lot of food sent in. Pies, cakes, salads, cookies. 2 canned hams.

A large funeral. Lots of flowers.

Vern looked very nice.

Fine snow. Ground white. D. sick all nite. Her stomach & bowels. I didn't hear her.

I took sick in P.M. I in bed all day.

Ever where glare of ice. We didn't sleep too good. My pep has left me.

D. & I out to cemetery toward evening. Flowers frozen. We are alone tonite.

D. still writing thank you notes. Second skift of snow. Washing & we ironed some.

Clarence took Linda back to Normal.

We are resting up. Picking up Christmas decorations.

Played Scrabble and watched old year out.

Cloudy all day. Most of ice & snow gone. Birds beginning to eat out of new feeder.

Little sun.